EXTRAORDINARY
ERNIE
& MARVELOUS
MAUD

EXTRAORDINARY ERNIE & MARVELOUS MAUD

Frances Watts
Illustrated by Judy Watson

Eerdmans Books for Young Readers

Grand Rapids, Michigan / Cambridge, U.K.

First published 2008 in Australia by
Australian Broadcasting Corporation
This edition published 2010 in the United States of America by
Eerdmans Books for Young Readers
an imprint of Wm. B. Eerdmans Publishing Co.

Wm. B. Eerdmans Publishing Co.
2140 Oak Industrial Dr. NE, Grand Rapids, Michigan 49505
P.O. Box 163, Cambridge CB3 9PU U.K.

www.eerdmans.com/youngreaders

Manufactured at Versa Press, East Peoria, Illinois, USA,
in February 2010; first printing

10 11 12 13 14 15 16   7 6 5 4 3 2 1

Library of Congress Cataloging-in-Publication Data

Watts, Frances.
Extraordinary Ernie and Marvelous Maud / by Frances Watts;
illustrated by Judy Watson.
p. cm.
Summary: Ten-year-old Ernie is thrilled when he wins a contest to be
trained as a superhero, and although he is disappointed that his sidekick
is a talking sheep, just looking at his costume makes him feel heroic.
ISBN 978-0-8028-5363-9 (pbk. : alk. paper)
[1. Superheroes — Fiction. 2. Sheep — Fiction. 3. Humorous stories.]
I. Watson, Judy, 1959- ill. II. Title.
PZ7.W3355Ext 2010
[E] — dc22
2009030446

For Extraordinary David
and
Brilliant Belinda
— *F.W.*

For Ali and David,
who trusted in my tortoises,
and for Jack
— *J.W.*

ONE

Ernie Eggers was late for school. And it was all the fault of The Daring Dynamo. Ernie was a big fan of The Daring Dynamo, who was everything a superhero should be — and everything that Ernie wasn't. The Dynamo was daring, obviously. And dashing. He was brave and strong. He never tripped over his own feet. He was never tongue-tied. His ears didn't stick out. And, Ernie guessed, The Daring Dynamo was probably punctual.

Unfortunately, the TV station that aired *The Daring Dynamo* was not so punctual. And because the show had finished late, Ernie — who couldn't

bear to leave his living room while the Dynamo was still in the clutches of the dreaded Count Crustaceous — was late too. Again . . .

Meanwhile, the four members of the Superheroes Society (Baxter Branch) were hanging around their headquarters on the alert for an outbreak of mischief. The ceiling fan whirred softly overhead, ruffling the yellowed newspaper clippings that were stuck to the walls. "Burglars Busted by Baxter's Bravest!" one declared, and "Reformed Rogue Hails Heroes" said another. There was a gentle hum of washing machines coming from the laundromat next door.

The president of the Superheroes Society, Super Whiz, was leaning back in his chair with his feet on the table, while Housecat Woman was curled up asleep in an armchair that sat in a patch of sun in the corner of the room.

Valiant Vera, watched by Amazing Desmond, was sorting the mail that had just been pushed through the slot by the door. "Bill, bill, free pizza offer . . ."

"I'll take that," said Amazing Desmond quickly, snatching the paper from her.

"Another bill . . . Oooh, here's something. It looks like a letter from the Superheroes Society International Headquarters. We haven't heard from HQ in years. I wonder what they could want?"

Housecat Woman opened her eyes in surprise, and Super Whiz swung his legs off the table and sat up straight.

"Give it to me," he said importantly. "I should be the one to open it. I *am* the president — and the brains — of the branch."

Valiant Vera passed it over, and Super Whiz tore it open and began to read, muttering under his breath.

Then he raised his eyes from the letter to the ceiling. "There's been a change in leadership. I suppose the new guys will want to poke their noses into everything." He turned his attention back to the letter. "It has come to our notice . . . blah blah blah . . . no new members recruited in years . . . blah blah blah . . . youth . . . grow and change to meet the needs of the twenty-first century . . . Ha!" Super Whiz slammed the letter onto the table in disgust. "They think we're has-beens — that's what this means."

"It's not our fault that things are quiet in Baxter," said Amazing Desmond. "I imagine villains know we're keeping a sharp eye on things, and that's why they steer clear."

Valiant Vera picked up the letter from the table and began to read. "They say here we should try to find new members. Maybe approach the local school. You know, it's not a bad idea," she said. "If we get some new members while they're young, we'll have plenty of time to train them. That way we'd be —" she read from the letter in her hand — "'ensuring the future of the Superheroes Society for centuries to come.'"

"So they want us to drag people off the streets and turn them into superheroes," snorted Super Whiz. "As if *anyone* could be a superhero. I presume HQ will still allow us to choose new members according to *our* high standards," he blustered.

"If we were to select some school students, for example, we would only want the brainiest ones from the top of the class."

"What about the top athletes?" asked Valiant Vera. "A superhero should be strong and brave."

Super Whiz nodded. "You're right," he said kindly. "We do need muscles to assist the brains. The only problem will be trying to choose our new members from among all the gifted young people begging to join our society. Of course, we can only accept the very best . . . Maybe we could make up some flyers and ask the principal to hand them out to the most intelligent students." He rose to his feet and began pacing around the room, his hand clasping his chin thoughtfully. "I know!" he said. "A contest! They shall compete for the honor of a place on our team."

"That's all very well," said Amazing Desmond, "but what's the prize?"

"What do you mean, what's the prize? I just told you — the honor of a place on our team! I can see the advertisements now: 'Do YOU have what it takes to be a superhero?'"

"Yes," said Desmond, "I understand that. But you still need to offer a prize. 'Win a fast car' or 'Win a luxury vacation' or something."

"Desmond's right," said Valiant Vera. "You can't have a contest without a prize. But I think it should be something a superhero could use. Now what does a trainee superhero need?"

"Help," yawned Housecat Woman from the corner. The others turned to look at her in surprise. Housecat Woman rarely stayed awake long enough to follow a discussion all the way through.

"What's wrong?" asked Super Whiz politely.

"That's what a superhero needs," Housecat Woman said. "Help to do all the things a super-hero does. Someone to share the exhausting workload." She gave another enormous yawn. "That's what I'd like, anyway," she said, and promptly fell asleep.

"Bingo!" said Amazing Desmond. "She's got it — a sidekick! There's nothing more certain to make a kid feel like a hero than their own faithful sidekick."

TWO

As he sprinted down the hill toward his school, Ernie could hear the bell ringing, and by the time he reached the school gate, the playground was deserted. Putting on an extra burst of speed, he leaped up the front steps two at a time and burst through the heavy wooden door into the school's main hallway. He was walking quickly down the hallway — he didn't want to get in trouble for running in the halls as well — when, to his relief, he saw a flash of color hurrying along ahead of him. Phew! He wasn't the only student running late! Then the other person stopped to look at the bulletin board halfway along the hallway, and Ernie saw that he had been mistaken.

It wasn't another student. It didn't seem to be a teacher either — too colorful. It was a short, slightly plump man wearing purple tights that sagged at the bottom, and an orange turtleneck that strained over his belly to meet the tights. A small purple cape was slung over his shoulders. Could this be a new drama teacher? Ernie couldn't think of another reason why a grown man would wear purple tights and a cape.

As Ernie watched, the man plucked a piece of paper from his bag and pinned it to the bulletin board. He then emptied the rest of the bag's contents into a trash can.

Ernie was so puzzled that he forgot to pay attention to his feet, which slipped out from under him. Next thing he knew, he was flat on his back and skidding along the hallway straight toward the stranger. Before Ernie could think to warn him, he had slammed straight into the man's legs. His schoolbag came to rest on his chest.

The man seemed surprised, but not upset.

Looking down at the boy tangled around his feet, he said, "Hello."

"Hi," said Ernie weakly.

"Where did you come from?" the man asked.

Ernie pointed back toward the door.

"Well, you're certainly light on your feet," said the man admiringly. "I didn't even hear you coming."

Ernie shrugged modestly, which is hard to do with a schoolbag on your chest.

"I'm Amazing Desmond," said the man, removing himself from the muddle of Ernie's limbs.

"Ernie," said Ernie.

"You're not some kind of athlete, are you, Ernie?" Amazing Desmond asked suspiciously.

"No," said Ernie honestly. He was rather flattered, though. No one had ever mistaken him for an athlete before.

Desmond studied him for a minute. "Athletes and A students," he muttered to himself. "Ha! We can do better than that. What we're looking for is guts and gumption — not the principal's pet." He

bent and pulled one of the pieces of paper from the trash can, and handed it to the boy. "You might be interested in this. Maybe I'll see you there." He set off down the hallway, whistling.

Ernie, still lying on his back in the school hall-way, began to read . . .

COMPETITION
OF THE CENTURY!!!

Superheroes Wanted!
Are you smart?
Are you swift?
Are you bold?
Are you brave?

If you answered yes to all of the above
questions, this is the chance of a lifetime!
Contest to join the elite **Baxter Branch**
(32 Main Street) of the world-famous
Superheroes Society will be held on
Friday afternoon at 4pm.

Winner will receive
free sidekick!

Ernie looked up and down the hall. Amazing Desmond was nowhere to be seen. Was this some kind of joke? He couldn't answer "yes" to a single one of those questions — but Amazing Desmond, who must be a superhero himself, seemed to think that he, Ernie Eggers, could become a superhero too!

THREE

It was already past four o'clock when Ernie hurried down Main Street looking for number 32. Passing a scruffy laundromat — number 30 — he stopped outside a florist — number 34. Looking behind him, he saw that he'd walked right past a vacant-looking shop.

On closer inspection, Ernie noticed that the shop's shabby brown door had "32" stenciled on it in small, neat numbers. He tried to peer through the storefront windows, but they appeared to have been papered over.

Ernie knocked.

After a few seconds the door was thrown open by a tall, thin man in blue tights. The letters "SW" were stamped in red across his bony chest.

He regarded Ernie sternly, taking in his rumpled shirt and dirty collar. "What do you want?" he asked.

"I'm here for the Superhero Contest," said Ernie.

"Oh," said the man. He gazed over Ernie's shoulder. "Is there anyone else with you?" he asked in a hopeful voice.

"No," said Ernie. "I don't think so."

"Oh," said the man again. "Pity." Then, taking a deep breath, he ushered Ernie into the room and began to speak very quickly in a jolly voice. "Welcome, welcome. I'm Super Whiz, and this is Housecat Woman and Valiant Vera. We're the judges."

Ernie said hello to Housecat Woman, who was in an armchair, and Valiant Vera, who was sitting on the far side of a large table. He couldn't see Amazing Desmond anywhere.

Super Whiz joined Valiant Vera at the table

and beckoned to Ernie, who moved to stand nervously in front of the table.

"Well, now," said Super Whiz, leaning back in his chair. "The fourth member of our little team, Amazing Desmond, is busy interviewing applicants for the sidekick position. That will be *your* sidekick, should you win this contest. Though I must warn you, the competition is very tough. Are you sure you're qualified to be here?"

Ernie was surprised. Amazing Desmond had been quite encouraging. "Well, I'm Ernie Eggers," he explained.

The superheroes looked blank.

Ernie paused as a thought struck him, and he looked around the deserted room. "Where are the other contestants?" he asked.

"Ah . . ." Super Whiz looked uncomfortable. "They . . . haven't arrived yet. But go ahead, Ernie. Tell us a bit about yourself."

"Oh, right." Ernie tried to stand up a bit straighter as he faced the judges. "My name is Ernie Eggers, I'm ten, and I'm very good at . . ." He paused again, trying to think of something,

anything, that he was very good at. "Football."

"Football? Now, that's interesting," said Valiant Vera. "What are your strengths? Speed? Stamina?"

Ernie slumped. "To tell the truth, I'm not that good at it myself. But I watch it on TV a lot, and . . ."

"What are your grades like?" interrupted Super Whiz.

"Um, they're not *that* good," confessed Ernie. "Just average, really."

"You do realize that this is the *super*hero contest, don't you? The *average* hero contest is next door." Valiant Vera gave a snort of laughter, and Housecat Woman let out a brief giggle.

"Oh. Okay. Sorry," said Ernie. He turned and walked toward the door.

Super Whiz rolled his eyes. "That was a joke."

Ernie turned back to face them. "Look, I know I'm not exactly super, but I really *want* to be. I'll work so hard — I can be here every day after school and on weekends — and I'm sure that with your help and lots of practice . . ."

Super Whiz held up a hand. "Please," he said, "spare us." He turned to Valiant Vera and began a whispered conversation.

Ernie could just make out snatches of it — "only entrant" and "one new recruit is better than" and "the principal must have rocks in his head."

Finally, the two superheroes turned to face him once more. "Welcome to the team," said Super Whiz with a sickly kind of smile. "You're a trainee superhero."

Ernie stared in shock. They'd accepted him. He'd won! He felt dizzy with pleasure. He'd never won anything before, and he'd never been picked for a team.

"So what are we going to call you?" Super Whiz asked.

"How did you all get your names?"

"They're based on our natural superpowers, of course. I'm a whiz in the brains department — obviously. Valiant Vera is brave and swift. House-cat Woman, well, when she was younger she was much more active: chasing, climbing, pouncing . . . And Amazing Desmond is, er — well the point is, what will *your* name be?"

"I suppose that depends on what my natural superpower is," Ernie said. "What is it, by the way?"

"Hmm, good question," said Super Whiz, looking Ernie up and down. "I have to say, nothing super springs to mind."

"Couldn't you, you know, *give* me some superpowers?"

"What, do you think we've just got some store-room of superpowers behind that door?" Super Whiz pointed to a door marked "Storeroom."

"Oh, don't be so mean, Super," said Valiant Vera. "You know it can take a while for powers to emerge."

"Maybe I could use some general sort of name," said Ernie. "Just until my natural superpowers kick in. How about 'Extraordinary Ernie'?"

"I'm not sure," said Super Whiz doubtfully. "It's not exactly accurate, is it?"

"Oh, go on, Whiz." The door had burst open to reveal the short, plump man Ernie had met earlier.

After a muffled conversation with someone behind him who Ernie couldn't see, Desmond quickly pushed the door shut.

"The kid looks all right to me," Amazing Desmond called out as he came over to them. "Surely we can stretch the truth a bit."

Ernie looked at him gratefully, but Super Whiz gave Desmond a dirty look. "The only thing being stretched around here is your tights," he said, poking Desmond in the middle. "I know you don't have super brains, strength, or speed, but you could at least try to stay in shape. And I've told you a hundred times," he added through gritted teeth, "don't call me Whiz."

"Whatever you say, Whi . . . I mean, Super," said Desmond cheerfully. "You know I can't get

to the gym as much as I'd like because of my bad back. So, I take it this is our winner." He clapped a hand on Ernie's shoulder warmly. "Excellent. I saw him down at the school earlier and suggested he come along. And have I ever found the perfect sidekick!"

"So what have you got for us, Desmond?" asked Super Whiz, rubbing his hands together.

"Something intelligent, I hope. An owl? A bit of wise counsel for our young friend here wouldn't go astray."

"No!"

"Perhaps it's a dear little monkey?" chimed in Valiant Vera. "Fast and nimble and great at getting out of tight spots . . ."

"Maybe it's a mouse?" purred Housecat Woman. "A plump, juicy, tasty mouse?"

"I know!" said Ernie. "It's a parrot! A parrot would be great." He imagined himself striding down the street in his superhero costume with a parrot perched on his shoulder, squawking "Make way for Extraordinary Ernie" and "Extraordinary Ernie to the rescue!"

"No, no, and no again!" cried Desmond. "I knew you'd never guess."

Bounding to the door, he flung it open and gestured grandly. "Well, here she is . . ."

There was a long silence, which was finally broken by the strangled voice of Super Whiz.

"Desmond, you idiot . . . That's a *sheep*!"

FOUR

"That's right!" said Desmond proudly.

There was another long silence, broken this time by the sheep herself. "What?" she demanded. "Haven't you ever seen a sheep before?"

"Ah, what's your name, dear?" asked Valiant Vera kindly.

"Maud," replied the sheep cautiously.

"Maud?" squawked Ernie, in the way a parrot would have done. "A sidekick called Maud? It doesn't exactly sound super, does it?"

"It was my great-aunt's name," explained the sheep. "My dad thought that if I was named after

her, she'd leave me all her riches in her will."

"And did she?" asked Ernie.

"No," said Maud sadly. "Sheep don't have wills."

"Oh, right. Well, who got all her riches?"

"No one. Sheep don't have riches either, since they don't have jobs. That's why I was so glad to see your advertisement for a sidekick. So, who's my hero? I suppose it's you, since you're the only one without a costume," she said, looking at Ernie with a sigh. "He doesn't look all that promising, does he?" she whispered to Super Whiz loudly. She turned back to Ernie. "So what's your name?"

"Ernie."

"Ernie? Well, if you don't mind my saying so, 'Ernie' isn't exactly the type of name to stop evil in its tracks either."

"I was named after an aunt too," Ernie said.

"Really?" asked Maud. "Was your aunt a man, then?"

"No," mumbled Ernie, embarrassed. "Her name is Ernestine. She's rich, but she's not dead yet."

"Oh, that's a shame," said Maud sympathetically.

"Look, I'm terribly sorry," said Ernie politely, looking around at the superheroes and then at Maud, "but I don't think this is going to work. It's just that — no offense — I was hoping for, you know, a *cooler* sidekick. Like . . . I don't know . . ." Ernie paused. Suddenly a parrot didn't seem all that cool either. "A big black dog or something."

"A big black dog?" echoed Maud. "That just shows your lack of imagination."

"Or a . . . a . . . a tiger," said Ernie desperately. "After all, what can a *sheep* do?"

"What can a sheep do?" Maud said. "What can *you* do?"

Luckily, she didn't wait for an answer.

"I'm a fast runner," said Maud. She trotted briskly up and down the length of the room a couple of times, hooves clattering on the wooden floor.

Valiant Vera and Housecat Woman both nodded approvingly.

"I can speak several languages."

Super Whiz looked impressed.

"And if I do say so myself, I have the gift of gab and a large helping of charm."

She winked at Amazing Desmond, who winked back.

They all looked at Ernie expectantly.

Ernie hesitated.

"Oh, that's right." Maud clapped a hoof to her woolly forehead. "You wanted cool. I've got just the thing." Maud stuck her nose into her woolly front and rummaged around for a few seconds. She emerged wearing a jaunty grin and a pair of black sunglasses. "Better?"

Ernie grinned back half-heartedly. He supposed being a superhero with a smart sheep for a sidekick was better than not being a superhero at all. "Sure."

"So what's your superhero name, partner?"

"Um, Extraordinary Ernie."

"Extraordinary Ernie? Oh, I like that. Good,

so we'll be Extraordinary Ernie and Marvelous Maud."

"Well," said Super Whiz, "our new recruits might not be *everything* I would have hoped for . . ."

"They'll be fine," said Valiant Vera firmly. "Now let's get you two outfitted."

She opened the door to the storeroom, and Ernie stared in wonder at racks and racks of suits and tights and capes in a dazzling kaleidoscope of colors and sizes.

"Baxter Branch used to have dozens of members," Vera explained, "so we needed lots of costumes. Take your pick."

Ernie scanned the racks eagerly. His eyes lit on a fluorescent green one-piece suit with a gold lightning bolt running down each arm. "That's a nice one," he said shyly.

Vera pulled it from the hanger. "It should look good with a green cape, I think," she said. She flicked through several hangers before finding what she wanted. She handed both suit and cape to Ernie.

"What about me? What about me?" Maud

was hopping from side to side in excitement.

Vera frowned at the racks of costumes. "I'm not sure we have anything in your size . . ." she began.

But Desmond, seeing the disappointment on the sheep's face, plucked something pink from a hanger. "Except this cape here," he said.

Maud brightened, and as Desmond fastened the cape around her woolly neck, she positively glowed.

FIVE

The first thing Ernie saw when he awoke the next morning was his green suit and cape. It was strange how just looking at it made him feel a bit extraordinary already.

He quickly dressed and bolted down his breakfast. This was one day he was definitely not going to be late!

Ernie arrived at the superheroes' office on Main Street just as Maud clip-clopped up the sidewalk from the opposite direction.

"Morning, partner," she greeted him. She looked nervous and excited. Ernie supposed that he looked the same. "You look super in your suit and cape."

"Hi, Maud," he said. "Thanks. Your cape looks very . . . dashing."

The sheep beamed. "Well, here we go — our first day."

Ernie opened the door.

The four superheroes were waiting for them. Valiant Vera looked at their costumes and — aside from a slight bagging at Ernie's knees — declared them a good fit.

Super Whiz waved Ernie and Maud over to the table where Amazing Desmond was already seated. Housecat Woman was asleep in the same armchair she'd occupied the day before.

Super Whiz then gave them a long lecture on the topic of Mischief, Havoc, and Chaos while Ernie did his best to look interested and Maud tutted intelligently. Amazing Desmond shifted restlessly in his seat. When Super Whiz started on the subject of Wrongdoing and Shenanigans, Desmond broke in.

"What do you say we begin a little on-the-job

training, Whiz?" he suggested. "There's nothing like a bit of hands-on experience."

Super Whiz looked annoyed — whether at the interruption or at being called Whiz, Ernie couldn't tell — but when he saw Valiant Vera bobbing her head in agreement, he sighed and stood up.

"Well, all right. I suppose they could do the Saturday patrol of the Main Street shops. Saturday's very busy," he explained to Ernie and Maud as they stepped out onto Main Street, "with everyone bustling and rushing. Tempers can become frayed. Accidents can happen. You need to be alert and aware. If any dangerous situations arise, report back immediately."

Ernie and Maud nodded obediently and set off.

The Main Street shopping strip was a small one, stretching just one block, which ran between the Baxter town hall at one end and the park at the other.

"It's strange," said Maud, as they walked purposefully down Main Street, which was crowded with Saturday morning shoppers. "When I woke up this morning, the first thing I saw was my cape — and just seeing it made me feel quite marvelous."

"That's exactly how I felt!" exclaimed Ernie, surprised to find that the sheep's thoughts were so like his own.

"So what made you decide to become a superhero?" asked Maud.

Ernie didn't know quite how to put it into words. "I guess I just wanted to feel like I was special," he said at last.

"I know just what you mean," said Maud. "I want to be more than just another sheep. Why, even when I was a little lamb, I . . . Ernie? What's wrong?"

Ernie had stopped dead in the middle of the sidewalk and was staring straight ahead. "There," he said.

"What is it?" asked Maud. "Wrongdoing? Shenanigans?"

"No, not that," whispered Ernie urgently. "It's Emma Plucker!"

"Where?" said Maud, craning her neck.

"Coming toward us."

"Oh," said Maud loudly. "The red-haired girl?"

"Shhh," hissed Ernie, for Emma Plucker was only a few feet away and seemed to be about to speak. "Just follow my lead, okay?"

"Ernie? Ernie Eggers? Is that you?"

"Yeah, it's me," said Ernie, blushing. "Hi, Emma."

Emma Plucker had never spoken to him before, even though they'd been in the same class since kindergarten. Sometimes Ernie suspected he might be invisible. Perhaps that was his natural superpower?

"Why are you dressed like that?" Emma asked curiously. Clearly, Ernie was quite visible in his fluorescent green suit.

"Oh, I'm a trainee superhero."

Maud was butting his knee. "Introduce me," she bleated.

"Oh, right. And this is my sidekick, er . . . Fang," Ernie said.

"Fang?"

"That's right."

"Your sheep is called Fang." It didn't seem to be a question.

"She's not a sheep, she's a sidekick. I mean, she *is* a sheep, but — she's trained in karate."

Maud scowled ferociously and kicked out with her back leg.

"Well," said Emma, "if I'm ever in trouble, I'll know who to call. See you, Ernie; nice to meet you, Fang." She waved a hand and strolled off down the street.

"Right, er, bye, Emma," said Ernie.

"Well," said Maud, as they watched Emma disappear into the distance, "she seems nice. Is she a friend of yours?"

"Oh, no," said Ernie, shocked. "She's very popular."

They continued their patrol of Main Street, walking up one side of the street — drugstore, bank, pet shop, laundromat, Superheroes Society, florist — then crossing the road and walking back down the other side — hardware store, toyshop,

fruit shop, convenience store, newsstand, book-
store, supermarket.

As the morning passed, the sun grew hotter
and hotter, and Ernie started to feel a bit prickly
inside his tight suit.

"I'm just going to stop at the store for a
bottle of water," he said. "Do you want anything,
Maud?"

"No thanks, Ernie. Oh, wait, yes — I'd love
some grape-flavored bubble gum."

"Okay." Ernie entered the shop and immediately

found his bottle of water, but he couldn't find any grape bubble gum. "I'll just be a minute," he said to the shopkeeper, putting the water on the counter.

He went to the door of the shop and called, "Maud! They've got strawberry and tutti-frutti, but no grape, so do you . . . Maud?"

She was gone.

Then Ernie heard a frantic bleating and saw Maud trotting around the corner of the supermarket as fast as her little legs could carry her — with a big black dog close behind!

"Maud!" cried Ernie, racing after them. "Hang on, Maud, I'm coming!"

He tore around the side of the supermarket and saw that the dog had cornered Maud by the dumpsters lining the back wall of the building. The dog was growling fiercely, teeth bared.

Maud's bleats had become whimpers, and her eyes were wide with terror. Her cape hung limply to one side.

Slowing to a jog, Ernie looked desperately about him for some kind of weapon. His eyes fell on an abandoned shopping cart. Perfect! Wheeling it in front of him, he began to run, and when he had gathered enough speed, he jumped onto the bar above the wheels.

"Here I come, Maud!" he bellowed.

The dog, startled, looked behind to see Ernie heading straight for him like a missile, his cape flying.

The dog fled, yelping in alarm, its tail between its legs.

Ernie put his feet back on the ground, and he and the cart skidded to a halt.

"Maud, are you okay?" he panted, rushing over to his trembling sidekick.

"Oh, Ernie," she whispered. "I thought . . ."

"Everything's all right now," said Ernie in a firm voice. "Did you see the way that dog took off?"

"Did I!" said Maud, some of the old spirit creeping back into her voice. "You sure scared him."

Ernie stood up, and Maud shook herself.

"You came at him like a rocket!" she said, pausing to give her cape a tug with her teeth. "And he took off like one," she continued.

Ernie listened to his friend praising his speed, daring, and ingenuity as they rounded the corner onto Main Street. Ernie Eggers was starting to feel just a tiny bit super.

SIX

By lunchtime the rush of shoppers had slowed to a trickle. Maud escorted an old man across the road, and Ernie helped a tired mother carry her shopping to the car, but they saw no Mischief, Havoc, or Chaos needing heroic intervention.

Finally Ernie suggested they stop for lunch. They bought cucumber sandwiches (Maud explained that she was a strict vegetarian) and took them to the park, where they found a cool spot in the shade of a large tree.

When they were done, Ernie gathered up their trash and took it over to the can on the far

side of the park. He was on his way back to Maud when he heard some familiar voices.

"Look! It's a celery stick!"

"Nah, celery doesn't have ears like that."

Ernie could feel those ears beginning to turn red. It was Lenny Pascal and his two followers, Wilbur and Gilbert. Wilbur and Gilbert weren't so bad on their own, but when they were with Lenny, some of his nastiness seemed to rub off on them. Privately, Ernie thought of the trio as Pascal's Rascals.

"Hey, look at this!" Lenny grabbed Ernie by the cape and used it to spin him around in dizzying circles. Then he let go suddenly and Ernie stumbled. Wilbur and Gilbert laughed, and when a shove of Lenny's knee sent Ernie sprawling on the ground, they laughed harder. They were still laughing as they ran off across the park.

Ernie burned with shame. He felt small and useless and not at all like a superhero. If he really were a superhero, he would have been able to stand up to those bullies. No, he said to himself, if he really were a superhero, the bullies never would have come near him in the first place.

It was a wilted bit of celery that was lying in the dirt when Maud came galloping over.

"Ernie, what happened?" she asked breathlessly.

Ernie sat up. "Pascal's Rascals," he said glumly. "They live on my street and they're always pushing me around, calling me names . . . I wish they'd just leave me alone," he finished angrily.

"Never mind," Maud said, attempting to dust him off with her hoof. "As we always say in the flock, names can never hurt . . ."

"Hey, listen, that's Emma's voice," said Ernie, looking up.

At the other end of the park, Pascal's Rascals had spotted Emma sitting on a bench by the pond reading a book.

As Ernie watched, Lenny grabbed the book and tossed it to Wilbur. Emma ran toward Wilbur, but he threw the book over her head to Gilbert.

"Stop it!" she was crying. "Give it back!"

"Those scoundrels!" said Ernie. "Come on,

Maud. Let's go!"

"Yes! What's the plan?" said Maud excitedly as Ernie leaped to his feet.

"I don't know yet," said Ernie as he took off like a shot. "We'll decide when we get there."

"I know!" said Maud, cantering smartly behind him. "You chase him as far as that tree there, then I'll leap out from behind that trash can and give him a karate kick to the knee, then . . ."

"Maud," said Ernie, "you don't know karate. I was making that up."

"Oh yeah," said Maud. "I forgot."

"Ernie!" said Emma as she caught sight of the trainee superheroes. "Help me!"

Lenny turned to see. "Ha! Look who's come to

the rescue!" he crowed. "It's Super Salad — and look: Ernie has a little lamb!"

Wilbur and Gilbert chortled.

"Lay off, Lenny!" said Ernie.

"Who's gonna make me?" sneered Lenny. "Hey, over here!" he called to Gilbert, waving his hands in the air.

Gilbert flung the book toward him, and just as the book touched Lenny's outstretched hand,

Ernie gave him a sudden shove.

"Hey!" Lenny shouted.

Lenny stumbled backward, right into Maud, who rammed all her woolly bulk hard into the back of the bully's knees.

"Wha . . . ?!" Emma's book flew from his grasp, and his mouth gaped as he teetered backward and tumbled into the pond with a loud splash.

A family of ducks immediately circled him, quacking their complaints loudly.

Wilbur lunged for the airborne book, but Ernie was too quick for him. He stuck out his foot, and the lunging Wilbur fell heavily, the book landing in the dirt beside him.

Ernie spun around to deal with the remaining bully, but Maud was already on the case. Eyes narrowed, her gaze fixed on Gilbert, she was pawing the ground like a bull. With a low, gruff bleat she lowered her head and charged, hitting the boy squarely in the stomach.

"Oooph!" he groaned as he fell, the wind knocked out of him.

Lenny, with the angry ducks still squawking

at him noisily, dragged himself dripping from the pond and took off across the park. Wilbur and Gilbert, groaning, lumbered after him.

Hands on hips, Ernie gave a satisfied nod, then bent and plucked Emma's book from the dirt. He carefully wiped it clean on his cape and presented it to its owner.

"Thank you, Ernie," she said. "And you too, Fang. You were both fantastic."

Ernie and Maud grinned at each other.

Then Ernie cleared his throat. "Actually, Emma, Maud's name is Maud — not Fang. I just made that up so she'd seem cooler." He flushed with embarrassment, then corrected himself. "That's not quite true either," he confessed. "I was trying to make *myself* seem cooler. Maud doesn't need any help. She's already the coolest person — I mean sheep — I ever met."

Emma tilted her head to one side and looked at Ernie thoughtfully. "Do you know what, Ernie? I don't think you need any help either. You're pretty cool too." Then she hugged her book to her chest and ran off across the park.

Ernie and Maud followed slowly.

"She's right, you know," Maud told Ernie. "You *are* cool. Why, on your very first day as a superhero you saved my life *and* defeated three bullies."

"*We* defeated those bullies," Ernie said. "I couldn't have done it without you, partner."

"Thanks, partner!" said Maud. She clicked her

hooves together happily and began to skip across the park toward Main Street.

Checking first to see that no one was looking, Ernie gave a little skip himself before jogging after her.

SEVEN

The four members of the Superheroes Society (Baxter Branch) were drowsing in the rays of afternoon sun that streamed through the dusty top windows of the storefront when Ernie and Maud burst through the door of 32 Main Street. They both started talking at once.

"There were these three bullies . . ." Maud began.

"Pascal's Rascals," panted Ernie. "They pushed me over, and then they were throwing Emma's book around!"

"But Ernie gave one of them a big shove," said

Maud, heaving her body to one side in demon-stration.

"Maud stared one down like a ferocious bull," Ernie broke in, "then charged him . . ."

"And the dog, Ernie, don't forget the enormous, vicious dog that had me cornered!" Maud reminded him.

"Just a minute, just a minute," said Super Whiz, holding up both hands to silence them. "Slow down and start at the beginning."

"Yes, it sounds like quite a story," said Valiant Vera.

"Be quiet, you two," said Amazing Desmond. "Let them speak."

Even Housecat Woman sat up to listen as Ernie and Maud related the day's adventures. The superheroes were full of admiration, and Ernie and Maud found that their storytelling was punctuated with praise.

"A shopping cart, eh? Good thinking, Ernie!" said Super Whiz heartily. "That's brains for you."

"Charged him like a bull, did you, Maud?" said Valiant Vera. "You see, it certainly pays to be daring and fleet of foot."

At the end of their recital, Amazing Desmond beamed proudly. "What did I tell you?" he said. "I knew these two had what it takes as soon as I laid eyes on them!"

"This calls for a celebration," Valiant Vera announced. Bustling over to the kitchen area at the far side of the room, she pulled a bottle of lemonade from the fridge. She divided it evenly between six old, chipped coffee mugs, and Desmond passed them around.

"To Extraordinary Ernie and Marvelous Maud," said Amazing Desmond, holding his cup aloft.

"Hear, hear!" the other three cried as Ernie and Maud tried to look humble.

"A speech might be in order, I think," said Super Whiz, clearing his throat.

"If you must," said Desmond. "But please make it a short one, Whiz."

Super Whiz shot him an icy glare.

"Ahem. Rarely has such courage . . ."

The speech promised to be a little longer than

Desmond was hoping for.

"... and it goes to show that teamwork, as these two fine youngsters have demonstrated..."

But Ernie didn't mind. No one had ever made a speech about him before.

"... facing challenges head-on, overcoming obstacles..."

He let the sun's rays wash over him. Next

to him, he could see Maud smiling softly as the golden light glowed on her fleecy curls.

"... So I am pleased to say with confidence that the future of the Baxter Branch of the Superheroes Society is assured!"

Ernie turned to Maud. "Being a superhero is marvelous," he whispered.

"It's extraordinary," she replied.

Acknowledgments

I would like to thank Brilliant Belinda Bolliger and Magnificent Jeanmarie Morosin of the Superheroes Society (ABC Branch), Wonderful Judy Watson and Extraordinary David Francis — all of whom would be right at home in Baxter.

— *F.W.*

About the author

Fearless Frances Watts is the author of *Kisses for Daddy* and *Parsley Rabbit's Book about Books*. She also works as an editor, and as the servant of a lazy cat. Frances likes traveling, cheese, and ducks, and dislikes ferocious dogs and having cold feet. Although her natural superpower has not yet emerged, she did once rescue a horse from a fire.

About the illustrator

Jittery Judy Watson has been a chicken all her life. She has illustrated several books for children, some of them quite terrifying. Her most frightening project so far was drawing the fearsome tiger for the Aussie Nibble *Tim & Tig*. Drawing the pictures for *Extraordinary Ernie & Marvelous Maud* sometimes caused her hand to tremble. This may explain many of the wobbles in her illustrations.

By the way, she is very impressed that Fearless Frances has rescued a horse.

Coming Soon

Ernie & Maud

The Middle Sheep

The adventures of Extraordinary Ernie and Marvelous Maud continue . . . but what — or *who* — is making the usually cheerful and dependable Maud so grumpy? And why are she and Ernie arguing all the time? It seems to Ernie that being his sidekick just isn't important to Maud anymore. Then Valiant Vera says that if the two trainee superheroes can't work together, they will be thrown out of the Superheroes Society! Ernie and Maud must learn the value of teamwork (and how to get a sheep out of a tree) before it's too late.

Ernie & Maud

The Greatest Sheep in History

Extraordinary Ernie and Marvelous Maud are back! Ernie and Maud are thrilled to be attending the National Superheroes Conference with the other superheroes from Baxter. But when the conference is disrupted by Chicken George — the most terrifying and villainous chicken anyone has ever seen — it will take more than just an ordinary superhero to save the day.